Khamoshi

Compiled By

Sanjay Naik & Aayush

Book Benchers

AELAY PUBLICATION

A dream come true for every writers out there. We spot every possible problem for the writers, help in rectifying them and guide them towards the best outcome. We make sure to understand your needs, dreams and expectations, and nourish them with our services and stop not until we fulfill your dreams. The writers have a right and freedom to choose what they want here. They have us to guide them through the hardest path until the end. Believe in us.

Aelay Publication - by a writer for the writers.

BOOK BENCHERS

Book Benchers is the affiliate of Aelay publication.
Both the publication is handled by Astro.
Aelay plays the role of publishing solo books.
And Book Benchers is epically for publishing anthologies.

Book Benchers have 2 different teams.

1. Tamil
2. English/Hindi

Never mind what our main motive is to help all the budding writers, who are seeking for their dream of publishing their own book to come true.

We are there to help out everyone.
In guiding for starting up with your carrier in compiling until finishing up your full book.

COPYRIGHT

Design And Executed by

aelay Publish.com

ISBN : 978-93-91423-72-8
Page : 119

ACKNOWLEDGEMENT

Acknowledgement is essential to boost up passion, making person more valid and precious, giving the team a great progress that makes worth.

We would like to use this opportunity to thank each and everyone who all the people involved in this book and, more specifically, to all the co-authors. Without your support, this book would not have become a reality.

We would like to thank each one of the authors for their contributions. Our sincere gratitude to all who contributed their time and expertise to this book.

We wish to acknowledge the valuable contributions of the Publication regarding the improvement of quality, coherence, and content. Last but not the least, we would like to extend our gratitude to parents and friends who have been a huge support through the book.

DISCLAIMER

This Anthology is a work of fiction. Our editors have tried their best to avoid any sort of plagiarism and the proof-readers have done their job of proof-reading best on their part to expertise the book with unplagiarized and original content. Still if any appropriation detected, the editorial team is no where responsible, the writer is solely responsible for such acts. We have well guided our co-authors to submit their original write-ups.

FOUNDER

IRUDAGA ASTRO

Irudaga Astro, From Tirunelveli, Founder of Aelay and BB (Book Benchers)

He had completed his BE.

He has written 3 Tamil poetry book's which hits the top list on social media!

His main aim is to allow the writers to publish their words as their book rather than just Posting them on Insta.

LINK AND POSTER MAKER

CATHERINE ASMI T

Catherine Asmi T, From Tirunelveli

She has completed her M.Com

Her passion is Drawing and Designing.

TEAM HEAD

She is a passionate writer from Chennai. Writing makes her pressure go away. She had played the role of co-author for more than 100+ Antho's.

She would like to thank her parents and her Loveable Brother for supporting her rather than stopping her from what she wanted to do! For being the main reason for achieving her dreams. As well as for standing beside her in all the ups and downs.

Whenever she feels like she needs to get out of her stressful timing or feels like she needs peacefulness, she starts to paint, she would never mind sitting in the same place for so many hours when it comes to her painting. She believes that anyone could hurt her, But never her books could!!

Catch her in Insta and FB

Insta: @theinnocentheart

FB: KA. PARINASRI

Index

28. Ashok Gangwar
29. Bhawna Mehta
30. Naveen Bhardwaj
31. Gargi Ghosh
32. Rozy Paul
33. Anusha Sathia
34. Darshini M
35. Poetry Khakholia
36. Tahreem Afzal
37. Aayushi Khedia
38. Srija Sadhukhan
39. Ankita Mishra
40. Deesha Soni
41. Ankita Nahar
42. Dr Aditi Dev
43. Priya Singh
44. Gajal Tayal
45. Yogesh Gurjar Chinu
46. Kajal Bhargav
47. Srushti Suman
48. Unnati Sawant
49. Karthik N

Sanjay Naik

(Compiler)

Sanjay Naik is from Kharagpur State of West Bengal. He is an Economics graduate (Hons), a writer from the heart and passionate about singing. Through the platform of anthology, he wants to spread love & positivity among his readers and wants to heal his readers' hearts with his magical words. Sanjay is at utmost peace when he pens his emotions. He believes that the power of his words, will heal the wounds of many readers. Till now he has participated in 500+ anthologies as a Co-author. He is a Compiler of 100+ anthologies. Some of his great works are:- "Self Happiness", "Scream", "Sarang". Instagram:- @the_poetry_wo

नाम !!

तेरे नाम का ज़िक्र आते ही उलझ सा जाता हूं
पढ़ता हूं उस खत को खोलकर अतीत
का किस्सा सुलझाता हूं
वक़्त हंसता है मेरे कारनामों को देखकर
सबकी नज़रों से कैसे खुद को बचाता हूं।

एक डर बैठ चुका है ज़हन में मेरे
दूरियों से रिश्ता निभाता हूं
कभी गौर फरमाकर देखता था
अब आंखें चुराता हूं
तेरा नशा कुछ अलग था जो उतरा ही नहीं
जब भी सोचता हूं बस मचल सा जाता हूं।

राह चलते मुसाफिरों से तेरा पता पूछ डालता हूं
दरवाज़े पर होते हुए भी ना खटखटाता हूं
फिलहाल सदमे से अभी बाहर आया हूं
फिर भी तस्वीर देखकर दिन गुजारता हूं।

Aayushi

(Co- Compiler)

Aayushi is from Purnea, Bihar and is a Physiotherapist by profession. She pours her heart on the paper and loves to scribble on it. She is fond of singing, dancing and dreams of being an artist. She believes that pen and paper are the best friends in one's life with whom one can share whatever they want and they won't ever judge you. Ig:- @compiling_mind_thoughts

खामोश लव्ज़

जहाँ एक ओर रात के अंधेरे में चारो तरफ खामोशी थी

वहीं दूसरी ओर न जाने क्यों दिल की धड़कने तेज़ थी।

साँसों में रफ़्तार थी पर बिल्कुल भी आहट न थी।

मैं अपने अंदर बहुत कुछ दबाय बैठी थी,

वो कह रहे थे 'जो बोलना है बोलो", मैं फिर भी खामोश थी।

शायद वो सही वक़्त था पर मैं तैयार नहीं थी।

बहुत कुछ था बताने को पर मैं अपने जज़्बात छुपाये बैठी थी।

रात गहरी होती गई और खामोशी बढ़ती गई

दोनो चुप थे पर फिर भी हमारी चुप्पी में बेइंतहा मोहब्बत थी।

HAR DEEPANSH BAHADUR SINHA

He is Har Deepansh Bahadur Sinha . He belongs to Lucknow,UP. He is a research scholar of Oceanography and has done masters in Geography from National Post Graduate College. Completed his schooling from Study Hall. His hobbies are art , listening to music , cooking & loads of driving. His interest areas are Astronomy, Writing, Photography & Travelling a lot. Ig:- @Deepansh_sinha

An Afflicted Story

It's a picture of a couple
Who were supposed to hustle,
In which one focused on chemistry
And other was full of mystery.

To normalize he made numerous sacrifice
But she never ever compromised,
Finally he was the one who struggled
She made his life completely puzzled.

Suddenly the bond got shattered
Meanwhile feelings also got scattered,
For her he was just a toy
Since she was dating another boy.

This lad didn't have any other choice
Also he was unable to listen his voice,
Still she didn't realise her mistake
His emotions were got extremely betrayed.

Every story does not have happy ending
Loads of people are still suffering,
So beware and make a wise connection
Who truly loves you and shows devotion.

PIYUSH KUMAR

पियूष कुमार यह एक अच्छे और बेहतरीन लेखक के रूप मे जाने जाते हैं l इनका निवास स्थल झारखंड राज्य के धनबाद जिले के अंतर्गत हैं जो की इनका कर्म भूमि और जन्म भी हैं । वर्तमान मे यह विश्वविद्यालय में हिंदी के प्रवक्ता है l यथावत इन की सभी रचनाएं पाठकों के ऊपर एक गहन छाप छोड़ती है l इनका मानना है रचना कभी मृत्यु को प्राप्त नहीं होती है रचना कभी ना कभी , किसी न किसी रूप में किसी न किसी से अपने आप को जोड़ लेती हैं l Ig:- @piyush_21011995

न जाने कब तक इस दुनिया का बोझ मैं बनता जाता..
न करता खुद से शिकायत तो खामोश हर दम रह जाता..
शिकायत पहले ये है कि क्यों खुद को मैं नही पहचाना..
दुनिया से दो-चार कदम क्यो हमेसा से पीछे रह जाता..
भरी महफ़िल में भी हर दम अपने को अकेला क्यों पाता..
मुस्कुराहट के पीछे का दर्द मुझमे हमेशा क्यों दिख जाता..
न जाने कब तक इस दुनिया का बोझ मैं बनता जाता..
न करता खुद से शिकायत तो खामोश हर दम रह जाता..
आजाद हु घर से पर, मन से आजाद क्यो नही हो पाया..
छोटी -छोटी बातों से क्यों मैं, दिल मे जहर घोलता आया..
सब मेरे साथ थे पर,क्यो मैं उनसे दूर हो पाया..
खुद का ही होकर क्यों मैं,खुद को दुख दे पाया..
न जाने कब तक इस दुनिया का बोझ मैं बनता जाता..
न करता खुद से शिकायत तो खामोश हर दम रह जाते।

HARSHITA VERMA

Co-author Harshita Verma is a writer from Lucknow. She has completed her graduation in commerce stream. She has been writing poetry for the last few years as her passion. She wants to be a novelist in future. Ig:- @0___hsh

Truth

Hiding the emotions from the whole world
Is it forbidden or it is the fear of being judged
Hiding in the crowd of elite society
Is it the fear of finding the true self
Hiding the real face and the mentality
Is if the choice of deception or the society had made you so
Hiding the sorrows and pains of life
Is there no one to see through or realise the truth.
Live life like it is the only chance you have
To know yourself and the one who is always there with you
To accept yourself the way you are and love the true you.

RAHUL VERMA

युवा हिंदी लेखक राहुल वर्मा, दिलवालों के शहर दिल्ली से ताल्लुक रखते हैं। इन्होंने मास्टर डिग्री कंप्यूटर साइंस में पूरी की है। फिलहाल राहुल जी संघ लोक सेवा आयोग आईएएस परीक्षा की तैयारी कर रहे है। राहुल जी कोई पेशेवर लेखक तो नहीं है फिर भी थोड़ा बहुत लिखने की कोशिश करते हैं। इनके ख्याल में एक लेखक अपने ख्वाबों को पूरा करता है, अपनी कलम से निकले हुए हर एक शब्द के जरिए और लोगों के दिलों तक पहुँच ना उसका सपना होता है। आप इन्हें फॉलो कर सकते हैं इंस्टाग्राम पर @rv.0711

मेरे दिल की कल्पना

जब समुन्दर की गहराई में डूबने का मन होता है।
तो मैं आपकी लहराती जुल्फों में कहीं खो जाता हूँ।।

जब तन्हाई मुझे अकेलेपन का एहसास करती है।
तो मैं आपकी खूबसूरत यादो में डूब सा जाता हूँ।।

जब आसमान में चांद सितारों को साथ देखता हूँ।
तो मैं अपनी हसीन मोहब्बत पर गुमान करता हूँ।।

जब कभी गुलाब की पंखुड़ियों को महकते देखता हूँ।
तो तुम्हारे चेहरे की कशिश को दिल से याद करता हूँ।।

जब कभी मेरा दिल तेजी से आपके लिए धड़कता है।
तो हर पल आपकी मौजूदगी का एहसास करता हूँ।।

- Rahul Verma (RV)

LIPSA DABHI

She is lipsa dabhi. She is Author and also good Co-Author. She is eighteen years old, she is student of the computer engineering.She is extraordinary person. She is always good leader. Her mam mrunal prajapati is her inspiration person and also her motivater, her friend chetna raval also supported to her and her mom manisha ben and her father nilesh bhai also supported to her for anytype of her creativity. She also wrote poems, short stories, shayries. Her writing skills almost very well and her creative collections are always best. Ig:- @__lipsa__dabhi__0829

“ खामोशी ”

खामोश सी रहती हूँ आज मैं,
उस खामोशी का हकदार तू ही हैं,
दूर सा क्यां चला गया मुझ से तू,
ए दिल खामोशी से दोस्ती कर बैठा,
कुछ फ्रकँ नहीं अब किसी भी बात का,
खामोशी ही तन्हा कर गई हैं मुझे,
खामोश से ए दिल का कोई ना सहारा,
पर खामोशी के साथ निड़र हो के जीना आज,
मुझे बेहतरीन तरीके से जीना हैं,
लिए खामोशी को हरपल साथ,
खामोश हैं तो क्यां हुआ जिंदा तो हैं,
खुद के हवाले बैठे हैं आज हम,
खुद ही खामोशी के साथ जीएगे यूँह,
खामोशी एक दोस्त हरपल साथ देती हैं ।

MOHAMMED NIYAZ

मायानगरी मुंबई के रहने वाले मोहम्मद नियाज़ एक ड्रॉप-आउट इंजीनियरिंग स्टूडेंट है। शायरी की दुनिया में इनहोने अपना कदम साल २०१३ में रखा था। इनकी कई सारी शायरी फेसबुक और इंस्टाग्राम पर काफी मनोरंजीत करती है। यह भविष्य में एक राइटर बनना चाहते है। आप इनहे फेसबुक (Mohammed Niyaz) और इंस्टाग्राम (niyazsks) पर फॉलो कर सकते है।

(मेहबूब का दीदार)

मग़रिब के वक़्त वह छत पर खड़ी थी।
आसमानों की तरफ उसकी नज़रें लड़ी थी।

मैं आया देर से क्या उसकी सांसें थम गयी थी।
मुझे देख वह जैसे हैरत पड़ी थी।

हाथ चूम कर उसका मैंने उसको तस्सल्ली दी।
माथे पर लगे एहसास की तजल्ली ली।

अज़ान की आवाज़ के साथ हमने दुआ की दरकार की।
अमन और सलामती की खातिर पुकार की।

फिर आसमानों में झलक चाँद की नज़र आयी।
माहे रमदान के खुशियों संग ईद का नूर ले आयी।

दिल झूम उठा हम दोनों के दो जहानों का।
मिल गया एक बहाना गले से गले लगाने का।

यादगार रहा मेरा तुम्हारा वह मुक़म्मल लम्हा कई बार।
मन्नतों में मिला जन्नतों जैसा "मेहबूब का दीदार"।

SONALI MEHER

Hey readers....!! She is Sonali Meher. From - Nuapada, Odisha, India. Currently pursuing for the degree of BAMS at Sri Sri nursingnath ayurveda medical College and RI. She is a Doctor by profession and writer by passion. She started writing when a very special moments come in her life and now for her writing is hobby. The writing is the 3rd person in that way of expressing their feelings, emotions and love. Now get a platform to exploring her writing. Hope ! You guys like it. Ig:- @Sonalimeher124

पहली बार जब आपको मिली थी
आप भी थे मैं भी थी पर पास नहीं थे
दूर खड़े बस एक दुसरे को देखते रहे
आपको देख के ही एक पल में
मैं दिवानी बन गई

आपके बारे में सब जानने लगी
आपको देखने और सोचने लगी
दूसरो से छुप के आपसे मिलने लगी
आपसे बेपनाह इश्क़ हो गई

आप इतने अच्छे कैसे हो
ना चाहकर भी आपसे प्यार हो गया
आप इतने मासूम कैसे हो
की कुछ ही समय मे इजहार हो गया

पता नहीं आपने क्या जादू किया
आजकल बस खोई-खोई रहती हुँ
ना जागती हुँ ना सोती हुँ
बस हर तरफ आप ही आप हैं

SAJAL KULSHRESHTH

Sajal Kulshresth, founder / creator - nazm_x_alfaaz an upgrowing page specialized in creating and sharing words; never spoken but felt! He has been inconsequentially writing since past couple of years. Kulshresth, an avid dreamer who believes in Idolatry, has achieved sucess at various events as a scholar. He promises to be a part of literature till his words are not only heard but hunched too! Ig:- @nazm_x_alfaaz

गुज़ारिश

..

बस एक गुज़ारिश है आपसे।
आप रहना उस सोने की तरह,
जो ढल जाता है सांचे में।
रहूं मैं उस सांचे जैसा ,
ढलो आप जिसकी आस में।
आज हकीकत को जाना
कि ज़िंदगी के हर किनारे पर साथ हो आप,
ये शब्द नहीं जज़बात है मेरे,
वरना दिल - ए - फ़कीर क्या जाने,
कि मेरी मुस्कान का असली राज़ हो आप।

He turned to his knees with a flower.
He : Te amo!
She : Te amo, mi amor!!
And they lived happily forever and ever!

SHASWAT SOURAV SAHOO

Shaswat Sourav Sahoo, is an eighteen-something adventurer who grew up traversing the wonders through the pages of metaphors. He fell in love with books and never reverted. Today he is pursuing his studies and living a clichéd life at NISER as an Integrated M.Sc. research scholar. He has been recently awarded with the Global Achiever's Award.When he is not sorrunded by words you can spot him fancying and pampering the dogs.He is a jovial kind of person revamping his past grief events into allured moments. He loves voicing his emotions and get it penned down.Another feather to his cap is his intense intimacy with taking shots. Nevertheless, he is also impassioned for painting, playing indoors, origami. He is looking forward his life being a polymath and pour on whatever he possesses within and wishes never to quell it. Ig:- @__shaswat__19

A Mile to Smile

My face cherished,
My mother caught me smiling,
Its the notification popped
That made this lunatic fantasized.
All of a while I started a mile,
A mile to the love of my life
"You are the soul of my body,
The Sirius of my azure,
Cure to my pain,
Remedy to my pistanthrophobia,
Honey to my bitter life,
Smile to my crying and
Happiness to my soul.
You are truth, you are peace,
You are effulgent ,
You are my sight,
You are miraculous,
You are the sunlight,
You are lavander,
You are bright."
One who has always got my back
The one who never leaves me
Neither in my odds nor my evens
The one whose single touch
Heals all my pain and sorrows
One who gives me hope to succeed
And scope to proceed
"You are eternal
You are dusk to my every painful night"

Lets cross the seven seas
And traverse beyond the world
And spare our entire life in an utopian island
Together and forever.
Thud,
Five fingers managed a place in my cheek
Pain suffused my face,
I saw my mother nagging
I came to back to reality.
Nonetheless, a day not so far
I will be in your lap, my love
In an Odyssey of appeasement
In an Utopian island,
Together and Forever.

KALAMKAAR

इनका नाम कलमकार है ये उत्तराखंड के रहने वाले है , मगर मेरठ में रह रहे हैं ! इनको लिखना और पढ़ना पसंद है! इन्होने 870+ अन्थोलॉजी में सेह लेखक के रूप में काम किया है और 750+ सम्मान पत्र जीते है! इनको लिखना और पड़ना पसंद है!इनकी रूचि लिखने में है!इनको कर्म पर विश्वास है फल से ज्यादा! इन्होने 20+पुस्तक में भाग लिया है सह लेखक के रूप में जो रिकॉर्ड के लिए गयी है! Ig:- @Kalamkaar51

संगीत

सुनते हैं जब हम तो तकलीफ दूर हो जाती हैं !
नींद बहुत अच्छी फिर आती हैं !
सुनने से संगीत नई ऊर्जा आ जाती हैं !
पुराने संगीत सुनने से उनकी अहमियत बताती हैं !
पुराने ज़माने की और हमको ले जाता हैं !
सुनते है संगीत जब खुद बा खुद गुनगुनाते है!
कुछ संगीत ऐसे होते है जो मन को बहुत भाते है!
इनको सुने बिना हम रह नहीं पाते है!
आजकल के संगीत मगर नये युवा को भाते है!
पुराने ज़माने के संगीत नहीं सुनना कुछ लोग सुनना नहीं चाहते है!
रैप लोग आजकाल सुनना चाहते है!
संगीतकारों से लोग नये नये संगीत सुनना चाहते है!
अगर मन को ना भाये तो संगीतकार के संगीत युवा नहीं सुनते है! ज्यादा
बीटवाले संगीत को युवा आजकल पसंद करते है!
संगीत सुनकर कुछ लोग अपनी सारी परेशानी भूल जाते है!
कुछ लोग संगीत के बिना रह नहीं पाते है!
कुछ लोग संगीत को अपनी पूजा मानते है!
कुछ लोग संगीत के घराने से ताल्लुक रखते है!
कुछ लोग संगीत बनाने के लिए पूरी पूरी रात जागते है!
मना दे उनको भी जिसका रूठा हो मीत!
ऐसा होता है संगीत!

©kalamkaar

PRACHI GUPTA

Prachi Gupta is a Passionate writer who loves to create her imaginary arts in a random canvas. She is pursuing her studies in BBA and lives in Allahabad known as The pure city of Sangam.

She loves to sing and watching movies in her free time. She is a shy and a open-minded girl at the same time For more information can follow her and contact:-
Prachiguptt0210@gmail.com

Ig:-@prachigupta3435 @prachi_gupta_210

WANTED TO DO

When you left me
I wanted to say something

When you made distance between us
I wanted to clear about something

When you was proving me wrong
I wanted to show you something

When you was covering your lie upon me
I wanted to fight with you

When you was shouting at me
I wanted to shout back at you

When you was trying to escape from me
I also wanted to get rid-off from you

When you was behaving good in front of all
I wanted to expose you
But it is all,
"I just wanted to do"

AGRIMA VIRAJ

She has completed her 18 years of adventurous life living in different corners of India and is currently preparing for the competitive exam NEET. She is highly determined to pursuit her profession as a DOCTOR. The writer within her awakened when she started penning down her boundless thoughts & emotions. She has co-authored more than 55 anthologies till now. She can solemnly portray herself to the readers through her writings and express the hidden contemplations within her. Being a writer she strongly believes that the magic of words and verse can change the insight of minds and souls as writing itself has changed her intellect and way of living life! To read her poems more, follow her on Instagram: @agrima_viraj YourQuote: Agrima Viraj You can also read her blogs on: www.theuntouchedmind.wordpress.com

लुका-छुपी

एक शांत ठंडी रात के दामन में कहीं छुपी हुई हूँ मैं
ढँढने मत निकलना मुझे, ना मिलूँगी कहीं भी मैं तुम्हे
धुंधले चाँद के साथ लुका-छुपी जो खेल रही हूँ मैं
एक शांत ठंडी रात के दामन में कहीं छुपी हुई हूँ मैं
सन्नाटे की सरल आवाज़ में बेसुध वहीं खड़ी हूँ मैं
ज़रा सी भी आहट ना करना, नज़र में ना आऊँगी मैं तुम्हे
एक शांत ठंडी रात के दामन में कहीं छुपी हुई हूँ मैं
ढँढने मत निकलना मुझे, ना मिलूँगी कहीं भी मैं तुम्हे

धुंध निशा की आगोश में झूलती कहीं बहती जा रही हूँ मैं
तारे टिमटिमाते नहीं पर जुगनु जगमगाते घेरे जा रहें हैं मुझे
चाँद को हौले से खिलकर फिर बादलों में गुम होते देख रही हूँ मैं
धुंध निशा की आगोश में झूलती कहीं बहती जा रही हूँ मैं
मधुर हवा के झोंकों पर सवार रात के नशे में लुढ़क रही हूँ मैं
फिक्र की झूठी तासीर लिए तुम सँभालने मत आना मुझे
धुंध निशा की आगोश में झूलती कहीं बहती जा रही हूँ मैं
तारे टिमटिमाते नहीं पर जुगनु जगमगाते घेरे जा रहें हैं मुझे

~अग्रिमा

ANAMIKA MAURYA

अनामिका मौर्या, मऊनाथ भंजन (उत्तर प्रदेश) की निवासी हैं। ये एक विद्यार्थी हैं और बी.एड. कर रहीं हैं। और इसके साथ ही इन्हें शायरी और कविता लिखने का भी शौक है, इन्होंने अपनी पहली शायरी कक्षा 12 में लिखा था। इनके शायरी और कविता को पढ़ने के लिए Instagram account- unique_anamika_maurya और fb account- Unique Anamika Maurya पर follow कर सकते हैं।

हाँ! बस ये बात दिल को समझाया आपने

खास तो कभी थे ही नहीं हम नजर में आपके
हाँ! बस ये बात दिल को समझाया आपने...

आओ ज़रा कह दो जो दिल में छिपा रखे हो
ख़ामोशीयों को क्यूँ ये जिम्मेदारी दिया है आपने...

तकलीफें ये ना थी कि अजीज़ कोई और है आपको
दर्द तो ये था कि हमसे ही क्यूँ छिपाया आपने...

नजर में ना आये आपके तो नजरअंदाज भी हुए हम
बहोत खूब! जो ये तरकीब आजमाया आपने...

ज़िक्र तो हमेशा यहां मोहब्बत की किया था हमनें
शायद यही वजह थी जो मुंह फेर लिया आपने...

मर तो गया था दिल फिर क्यों एहसास जगा दिया
अब समझ आया क्यूँ ये वहम दिलाया आपने...

खैर गलती मेरी थी जो ये वहम पाला हमनें
शुक्रिया आपका जो ये एहसास कराया आपने...

मोहब्बत ने भी नजराने में ग़म तमाम दिये
हाँ! बस ये बात दिल को समझाया आपने...

SHIVAM MAURYA

इनका नाम :~ शिवम् मौर्या यह गोरखपुर उत्तर प्रदेश से हैं।
ये दिल से एक लेखक और गायन के बारे में भावुक।
वह अपने पाठकों के बीच प्यार और सकारात्मकता फैलाना चाहता है और अपने जादुई शब्दों से अपने पाठकों के दिलों पर मरहम लगाना चाहता है।
शिवम सबसे ज्यादा शांतमय है
उनका मानना है कि उनके शब्दों की शक्ति, कई पाठकों के घावों को ठीक कर देगी। Ig:- @_as___writes_

“जिंदगी"

जिंदगी को समझने लगा हूं।।

ख़्वाब से अब ज़रा जगने लगा हूँ
जिंदगी को बेहतर समझने लगा हूँ ।

उड़ता था शायद कभी ऊँचा हवा में,
जमीं पर अब पैदल चलने लगा हूँ ।

लफ़्ज़ों की हमे ज़रूरत नहीं है,
चेहरों को जब से पढ़ने लगा हूँ ।

थक जाती हूँ अक्सर इन शोर से,
ख़ामोशियों से बातें करने लगता हूँ ।

दुनियाँ की बदलती तस्वीर देख कर,
शायद मैं भी कुछ कुछ बदलने लगा हूँ ।

नफ़रत के ज़हर को मिटाना ही होगा,
इरादा यह मज़बूत करने लगा हूँ ।

परवाह नहीं कोई साथ आए मेरे,
मैं अकेले ही आगे बढ़ने लगा हूँ ।

ABHISHEK SINGH

Hello my name is Abhishek Singh I am 18 years old I am basically belongs to Bareilly, Uttar Pradesh. Writing is his all time Passion. And I found peace in this & wanna be a good published Co-author. You can follow me on Instagram @mystri0us_sc0rpi0n If you enjoy my work so plz tell me i will giving my best

तुम नहीं जानती कि वह रातों को जगना तुम्हें देखना
और तुम्हारे फोटो को चुम कर सो जाना कितना सुकून देता है
मुझे, ये तुम नहीं जानती .. तुम
नहीं जानती कि कैसे तुम्हारी सांसे और आहे गरम लगती है
मुझे सर्द रातों में ये तुम नहीं जानती...
तुम नहीं जानती कि कैसे ख्वाहिश है पूरा जिंदगी बिताने की
तुम्हारी जुल्फों के साए में , ये तुम नहीं जानती...
तुम नहीं जानती कितने लड़के तुम्हारे लबो को तरसते है तुम
नहीं जानती तुम नहीं
जानती की कितने बादल तुम्हें छूने को तरसते हैं ये तुम नहीं
जानती... तुम नहीं
जानती कि इश्क क्या है, ये तनहा राते हैं, ये अधूरी बातें हैं ये
मचलती सांसे हैं यही तो इश्क
है मेरा यह तुम नहीं जानती ....
तुम्हें अलविदा कहने में इतना दर्द क्यों है..
गर्मी के मौसम में हवा कितनी सर्द क्यों है..
इन दोनों सवालों के जवाब में..
आखिर तेरा ही नाम क्यों है..
तुम्हें अलविदा कहने में इतना दर्द क्यों है...
आज मेरा दिल जख्मी है लेकिन साँसों में मगरूरी है..
कुछ बातें हैं जो बेकार है, लेकिन तुझे बताना जरुरी है..
आज तू ने नहीं पूछा हाल मेरा , लेकिन तबीयत मेरी अच्छी
है..
मुस्कान जरा सी झूठी है, लेकिन बातें मेरी सच्ची है..

आज तूने नहीं पूछा लेकिन फिर भी मैंने खाना खाया है..
आज सुबह तेरा कॉल नहीं था लेकिन मेरी माँ ने मुझे जगाया है.. शुक्रिया तेरा कि
आज राजा बेटा हुआ हूं फिर से...
इन बाबू ,सोना ,जानू से दूरी है, कुछ बातें जो तुझे बताना जरूरी..

S. SUGANTHI

Suganthi has been writing for over two years. She provides philosophical writings. Her educational background in English literature has given her a broad base for writings. Her books are available in Amazon Kindle named Heartly Sayings and Healing journey-11.
Ig:- @chum_moon

Title : tears

People hide their feelings from others but the tears in their eyes can't be hidden. It shows the truth. Hiding feelings won't you heal fast. Share your pain with others. Then only you can heal fast. Accept the reality and live the life. Don't hide your feelings with others because they stay inside you and hurt day by day. Most of them hide their feelings and sufer. Heal the pain by sharing with others or forget the mistakes of others. Life change, only when you heal your pain.

MANISHA S KAUSHAL

इनका नाम मनीषा कौशल है। झीलों की नगरी भोपाल की ये रहने वाली है। वर्तमान में ये श्री भवंस भारती पब्लिक स्कूल में हिंदी शिक्षिका के पद पर कार्यरत हैं। इन्हें लिखने का शौक बचपन से था परन्तु अपने शौक को कभी व्यक्त नहीं किया। कोरोना काल के अन्तर्गत मन में बसी हुई सारी बातें इन्होंने लेखन के द्वारा व्यक्त की। पिछले 15 वर्षों से ये बच्चों को हिंदी पढ़ाती आ रही है। लेखन क्षेत्र में ये और लिखना चाहती है।

Ig:- @Manisha Kaushal75

"मेरा पन्ना"

अजीब सी मोड़ पर आकर रुक गई है जिंदगी समझ में नहीं आता कि आगे क्या करना है। रिश्ते दूर होते जा रहे और मन में कड़वाहट भरती जा रही, एक ऐसे ही मोड़ पर आज मनु खड़ी है...सोच रही है की कैसे उलझे हुए धागो को सुलझाए। 27 साल पहले जब उसकी शादी हुई तब उसकी उम्र 21 वर्ष की होगी...सोचा था शादी के बाद सब कुछ बदल जाएगा.... बदला तो सही पर जैसा उसने सोचा था। उम्र में उसके पति उस से 12 वर्ष बड़े थे उनकी सोच और मनु की सोच में अंतर था। उनके घर में उनकी दो बहनें और उनसे बड़ा भाई डॉक्टर थे वो खुद भी सरकारी नौकरी में थे एक छोटा भाई ही था जो कुछ नहीं करता था। शादी के बाद मनु को पढ़ाई करवाई जिसके बाद वो अध्यापिका बनी लेकिन दोनों के बीच विचारो का पन्ना आज भी अधूरा है क्योंकि कही ना कहीं उनका अहम इस बात पर आता है कि मेरा मान सम्मान होना चाहिए ये अहम दोनों के रिश्ते के पन्ने को कभी पूरा नहीं होने देगा।

SONAL PRAJAPATI

I am Sonal Prajapati living in Delhi. Electrical Engineer by profession and writer by passion. I had been part of online writing contest and books like the cage of soul, jeevansathi, the inked solace, classy lassie, hope- a positive vibes, colleen warriors, soliloquy, twinkling versus, Nzare unke, love is everything, Incarnation and hope- faith & trust, love-a journal, friendship a book, kuch lamhe yaadon ke, satrangi barsaat, ishq ke raste, lines from the heart, Tu jo mere sath hai. Ig:- @Misswriter_

My world

My day starts from you and end on you.
Everyone loves me for my nature
But who I loved is all matter.
Clearing all pain that i have
Dancing with me in the rain
Holding my hands on way
I just closed my eyes & run away
Drinking tea in same cup
Taking our career in up
Fighting for me in the ring
He always pay for what I bring
A behind hug from him
Remind me of everything
U always make me pride
U are the one who never lied
Taking me with you on ride
He always stays on my side

JOYOUS JAYA RAUNIYAR

This is Joyous Jaya Rauniyar from Nepal .she writes everything she feels as it becomes listenable .Being co author of 50+ anthologies, author of 2 books, compiler of 6 anthology and brand ambassador of 2 books as well as 2 groups ; she want so much more to express. She is also BEST EMERGING AUTHOR 2021. Writing is her love which can never fade away . Happy Writing ,let's create a change through it. Follow her on YourQuote @Joyous Jaya Rauniyar. Ig:- @jaya_uncaptured

रिश्ते भी आज कल कितने नाजुक होगये है,
ज़रा शा हवा का झोका इसे मोड़ देता है,
वो हफ्तों से लिखी चिठ्ठीया आज ख़तम
कर उन्हें आश्चर्य करने वाली थी शाम को,
गलतफ़हमी के कारण रिश्ता यु सुबह ही टुटा,
1हमे ही आश्चर्य कर दिया उन्होंने,
एक पल मे ही .....

YASMIN AAMIR AMEEN

She is a housewife. A creative writer who has got her work published in newspapers and magazines in her city. She has also been a co-author in quite a few anthologies. She generally expresses her emotions through poetry. Ig:- @nobody_281195

Silence is the key!

One day i was sitting with my family and suddenly out of the blue we started discussing about silent letters in the English language. English is generally known as the funny language. This point made me curious and i researched on it. Hence i came to know a lot many things. Silent letters are the ghosts of pronunciations past. These are the letters in words that are not pronounced, but make a huge difference to the meaning and sometimes pronunciation of the whole word. Do you know 60% of the English words have silent letters in them which can cause all sorts of problems while spelling the word or looking for it in the dictionary. Silent letters aren't there to mess up with your brain. These letters help the readers in many ways.

Now i would like to let you all know what is the importance of these silent letters in the English language.

* They help you to spell correctly, write without any errors and boost your confidence.

* They help the reader distinguish between homophones (homophones are words with same sound but different spelling and different meaning). For example, in/inn, be/bee, no/know, not/knot and many more.

* A silent letter can help us work out the meaning of the word and also change the pronunciation of the word even though it is silent. For example, sin/sign, to/too, etc.

* There's a magic letter in the English language "e". If you add "e" at the end of the short vowel sound words it elongates the sound. For example, rid/ride, cap/cape, fat/fate, etc.

* Sometimes people might pronounce certain letters or they might not depending on their accent. For example, the "t" in "fasten" maybe pronounced or not.

*"H" is silent in a lot of accents. It is silent in some words from French - hour, honest, heir, etc.

* They show the origin and the history of the word (etymology).

So this is all about silent letters. If you hate spellings and if you want to learn and improve your spellings you can take interest in words, discover the logic in the spelling system and understand the history of words. Go on people! Have fun with this language! Good luck!

RAVISHANKAR NISHAD (ARVI)

यह रविशंकर निषाद है । ये शाखा :- तमनार, जिला :- रायगढ़ (छत्तीसगढ़) के निवासी हैं । इनका जन्म 19 जून 2000 में हुआ था ।। यह अभी इंजीनियरिंग कॉलेज में पढ़ाई कर रहे है । इनकी रुचि कविताएं लिखना है और यह किताबों के शौकीन भी है ।। Ig:- @arvinishad

Topic :- **फैसला हो गया**

ले मेरे प्यार का फैसला हो गया
तू मेरी हो गई मैं तेरा हो गया ।।
तू भी अनजान थी मैं भी अनजान था
देखते देखते क्या से क्या हो गया ।
तुझसे मिलकर दिलों पर ये असर हो गया ।
तेरे साथ हर राह सुहाना सफर हो गया ।
आखों ने आखों से किया इजहार
बातों ही बातों में तुमसे प्यार हो गया ।।
ले मेरे प्यार का फैसला हो गया ।।
तेंरे मेरे मिलन का ये असर हो गया
गमनुमा सा ये मंजर प्यार का मौसम हो गया ।
महकती फिजा हर तरफ
कलियां खिलकर अब गुलाब हो गया ।।
तू मेरी महबूबा मैं तेरा महबूब हो गया ।।
ले मेरे प्यार का फैसला हो गया ।।
Ravishanker Nishad (ARVI)

ANANYA P MISHRA

Myself Ananya P Mishra from Bhubaneswar, Odisha. I'm a student of English Honors. Believes in karma. Bookaholic. Want to set an example for this era that inspires others and me as well. Love dancing, designing and exploring new things. Self-love is priority. Always know your worth. Ig:- @ananya_payal191

Craving for her love-

His despair and grief and regret,
there was so much emotion churning
inside him that it was tangible and thick
in the air.
It rolled off him in waves
And then his touch became gentler
become more beseeching
almost as if he was begging her
not to deny him.
To offer him the comfort he seemed to crave, to touch
him back,

to hold him with same intensity and love.

ANKUR MISHRA

बातें अपनी दिल की इस कदर किया करते हैं,
जज़बात को बयां कोरे पन्ने मे किया करते हैं।

ये हैं अंकुर मिश्रा जो वर्तमान मे देवास मध्यप्रदेश मे कार्यरत एक उभरते हुए लेखक हैं जो कि जिंदगी और नौकरी का संतुलन बनाये रखते हुए अपने लेखन के शौक को जिंदा रखे हुए हैं। इनकी रचनाये पच्चीस से ज्यादा ई-बुक/किताबो मे प्रकाशित हो चुकी या होने वाली हैं। भविष्य मे ये अपनी सभी रचनाओ को खुद की पुस्तक मे संजोने का ख्वाब रखते हैं। इंस्टाग्राम मे आप इनसे अपने विचार ankdip2801 मे साझा कर सकते हैं

खामोशी

सुन नही सकते खामोशी को लोग सरे-आम है,
खामोश लब भी बोलते है बस समझने वाला हो ।

खामोशी को न समझना हर किसी का काम है,
अल्फाजों के राज खोलते है बस समझने वाला हो ।

खोज पाना नही चाहता ये एक ऐसा तामझाम है,
छुपे इरादों को टटोलते है बस समझने वाला हो ।

है स्वाद छिपे इसमे जो जज्बात के घुले जाम है,
स्वाद जज्बातों के घोलते है बस समझने वाला हो ।

दुनियादार के बाजार मे खामोशी का बहुत दाम है,
अपने गैरो के भाव तौलते है बस समझने वाला हो ।

खामोशी को बिना समझे कर देते लोग बदनाम है,
लोग न बोल के भी खौलते है बस समझने वाला हो ।

खामोशी के बेकरार दिनो की कभी न ढलती शाम है,
तसव्वुर के आलम टटोलते हैं बस समझने वाला हो ।

OM PRAKASH LOVEVANSHI "SANGAM"

आप राजस्थान के बाराँ जिले के देहलनपुर गाँव से आते हैं।आपकी "आओ-ना फिर से तुम" ,"कलम की गूँज"और "शब्दों की महक" पुस्तके प्रकाशित हो चुकी हैं। 50 से अधिक साझा संग्रहो में बतौर सहलेखक रचनाएँ प्रकाशित हुई है। 20 बार साहित्य पत्रिकाओं में रचनायें प्रकाशित हुई हैं।संगम पब्लिकेशन के आप फाउंडर हैं।insta id sangam_banna

सुनो! तुम चले आओ

कभी मिले थे हम
यहीं चंबल के किनारे
और अब जी रहा हूँ,
बस उन्हीं यादों के सहारे
ये यादें ताज़ा हो जाती हैं,
जब भी मैं वहाँ जाता हूँ।

वो लहरें, वो पंछी
सब के सब गवाह हैं,
तेरे मेरे मिलन के,
चंबल के किनारे बैठकर
बातें करना,मस्ती करना,
क्या ??
अब तुम्हारा मन नहीं करता
शाम को शांत माहौल में
प्रकृति के पास बैठने का ।
चंबल के हिलोरों की आवाज,
पंछियों के झुंड का कलरव
और मछलियों की अठखेलियाँ
ये सब कितना अच्छा लगता था
दुनियां से परे
एक अलग ही अनुभूति होती थी।
सुनो! तुम चले आओ-ना फिर से
मैं तुम्हारा इंतज़ार करूँगा....!!

DAKSHITA JAISWAL

Dakshita jaiswal is a 18 year old Management student. She is from Gonda, Uttarpradesh. Being a voracious reader and writer, She has organized multiple events and itself is a poet, storyteller, blogger and a published author.

She is the core team member of Happy hearts organization, an event organizing house. She inculcates high interest into the field of writing and have performed at various platforms. You can search her on Instagram @invoicer_dakshita_jaiswal.

{शीर्षक: तुझको कविता कहूँ, या खुद को शायरा......!}

नज़्मों में एक अश्क सा छोड़ा था,
अज्ञात दिशा में यू इश्क़ ने मोड़ा था,
जहाँ ज्ञात सैलाब में एक अज्ञात सा ख्वाब था,
दबी मुस्कुराहटों में उसकी छुअन का एहसास था,
जहाँ उसकी धड़कनों में धड़कते दिल का छिपा राज़ था,
ए ख़ुदा, ये इश्क और मुश्क में जाने कैसा शाज़ था,
जहाँ उसके लबों पर रूहानियत भरा , ऐतबार था,
इख्तियार में उसकी चुप्पी में छुपा कुछ सार था,
कुछ लम्हों में यून इस क़दर उसमें बसा मेरा संसार था
सही या ग़लत , जाने यह इश्क़ का कैसा वार था,
न दरिया और ना ही दायरा ,
न ज़रिया और ना ही कायरा ,
तुझको कविता कहूँ , या खुद को शायरा!
-दक्षिता!

PRAKASH TURIYA (RAGHUWANSHI)

Prakash Turiya, belonging from chhindwara, Madhya Pradesh. Education M.pharma, working as senior executive medical writer. Ig:- @light@Raghuwanshi

क्युं सताते ये पल हैं।

न जाने क्या आश हैं, कौन किसके पास हैं।
न जाने किसकी तलाश हैं, सब कुछ तो आसपास हैं।
क्या ये पल निःसछल हैं, क्युं सताते ये पल हैं।

आंधियों और तुफानो में, अपने से बेगानो में।
इन चलती हवाओं में, इन उत्खल नदियों की लहरों में।
क्या आने वाला कल विफल हैं, क्युं सताते ये पल हैं।

दम तोड़ता ये जीवन, अब नही रहे जंगल, ना रहे वन।
कुदरत की हवाओ में, जहर घुल गया फिजाओं में।
मानव रहे गया अब हाथ मल हैं, क्युं सताते ये पल हैं।

वृक्षों को रोपना हैं, इनकी कटाई को रोकना हैं।
हरियाली के साथ साथ खुशहाली भी बटोरना हैं।
क्युं रूहाना सा ये कल हैं, क्युं सताते ये पल हैं।

PRAKHAR RAGHUWANSHI

I am Prakhar Raghuwanshi from betul city of madhya pradesh and currently studying in class 12th, 15 years old. I have been involved in the field of writing specially poetry since last one year. Ig:- @prkhrrghuwnshi_1

"आत्म पुकार"

ज़िन्दगी के हर लम्हे को,
खुल के जीने का मन होता है,
पर कभी-कभी सहम जाता हूँ।

बन्दिशो को तोड़कर सारी,
आगे बढ़ जाने का मन होता है,
पर समझौता कर ठहर जाता हूँ।

बादलों के ऊपर जाकर,
आस्मां चीरने का मन होता है,
पर थोड़ा उड़ के सम्भल जाता हूँ।

ज़िन्दगी से परे, कहीं दूर,
गुम हो जाने का मन होता है,
पर हालाथो में ही ढल जाता हूँ।

ASHOK GANGWAR

Interests :- Writing Poems

Hobbies :- Video Games , Book Reading

From :- Karamchari Nagar, Bareilly , Uttar Pradesh

Aim :- To Become a Indian Naval Officer

Ig:- @ashok_19dec and @youth.wakeup

WORDS TO THE SOLDIER

APNI JAAN GAVANE KA,

KHATRA LE MA MOL RAHA HU, MAIN JUNG ME LADTA HUA JAWAN BOL RAHA HU,

NEEND AAYE BHOT BHAYANKAR, PAR PHIR BHI MAIN APNI AANKHO KO KHOL RAHA HU, MA BORDER PE PEHRA DETA SAINIK BOL RAHA HU.

MUJHE BHI HA APNE PARIWAR SE PYAR BHOT,

PAR MAIN APNE DIL ME KADHORTA KA DARWAJA KHOL RAHA HU, MAIN HAR PAL DESH KO UPAR RAKHNE WALA FAUJI BOL RAHA HU.

APNE PARIVAR KI AOR ZIMMEDARIYON KO, APNE DESH KE PRATI FARZ SE TOL RAHA HU,

MAIN DESH PE MARTA PAR PARIVAR KE LIYE JEETA SIPANI BOL RAHA HU.

DUSMAN KO YAAD KRKE,

HAR PAL MA KHAUL RAHA HU, MAIN US RAKSHAK KE ANDAR KA KHOON BOL RHA HU.

JISNE NIKALI AAKHRI SAANS DESH KE LIYE,

USKE SAMMAAN MEIN MAIN GOONJ RAHA HU

MAIN US SAHEED KI VIDAI PE PITTA DHOL BOL RHA HU.

#MYWORDS #ASHOKGANGWAR

NAVEEN BHARDWAJ

Myself Naveen bhardwaj a programmer by profession a lover of poetry maker and like reading books and audiobooks and he has telegram channel @TheNBbook insta I'd na.vin7832

There were the times we love them for who they are and accept them. But the bond we share is something cannot be hidden by anyone. When I am alone I talk to myself thinking that maybe somewhere in the middle of road or cross path I will meet you again and we start our conversation we had left before. But now that is all gone. Maybe we will meet on another time. Talking about our story we always had secret talk and long chatting the promise we keep that we are made for each other but you left me in the lurch without thinking what will happen with me. How I will manage to cope up with this. You told me you will never left me but see for a little fight you said good bye and never meet me again. These words are still roaming somewhere in my mind. I still can't find the answer of this question. Can you tell me what it was.

BHAWNA MEHTA

She is presently pursuing B.Ed from Guru Jambheshwar University,Hisar. She like to pen down her thoughts.She has written two Blogs and won Blog Competition also. Ig:- @bhawna_mehta04

ना जाने क्यूं रूठी सी हैं यह ज़िंदगी,
लगता हैं कुछ पीछे छूट रही हैं यह ज़िंदगी,
कभी हस्ते तो कभी गमों में बस जी रहे हैं ज़िंदगी,
ना गिला ना शिकवा किसी से,
खुद में मस्त हो कर गुजर रही हैं ज़िंदगी,
सबने बहुत कुछ सिखाया,
बस इसी खेल में व्यतीत हो रही हैं ज़िंदगी।

GARGI GHOSH

A girl who lives in BERHAMPUR, Murshidabad.she has completed her master's degree in English literature writing is her passion.she always wants to spread a positive vibe & LOVE at her society Ig:- @bong girl gargi 12

silence

Silence is not empty.
It's full of answers.
If you want success,
Work hard in silence*
Let success be your noise
Move in silence,
Only speak,
When it's time to
Checkmate.
Silence is the best answer.

GARGI GHOSH

ROZY PAUL

Her name is Rozy Paul.She belongs to the tea-estate called Dibrugarh,Assam.She has done M.A.in journalism.Her hobbies are reading,gardening and cooking.She likes travelling a lot.Her favourite quote is 'live and let live'. Ig:- @Writer_rozypaul

Heart talks: Heart often talks based on emotion.Feel like to go vacation after lockdown.If someone will take me I will surely go.Boring at home and same locked up when those days will come like free to go anywhere.

ANUSHA SATHIA

Anusha is a writer and a poet hailing from India. She is currently in high school. She has been writing since quite a few years and that has been her passion. She uses her positive attitude and tireless energy to encourage others to work hard and succeed and she writes because she enjoys expressing herself. For more of her work, please check out her Instagram handle: @_thelittletherapist

Do you ever have a moment

where you think to yourself:
I should have done
I really regret
I shouldn't have
I wished that
These are thoughts of the past
Those things that you did in the past
That you wished were different are gone now
You only have this moment and the future days to come
To finally do something
That you want to do

Don't let anyone stop you
You can do this!

DHARSHINI.M

She is dharshini from kovilpatti. She is pursing masters in English. She has huge interest in writing.she loves to share her thought and emotion through her writing.She has done many anthologies as co author. She has published a book named **'vox of mine '**.
Ig:- @dharshji_dharsh

Quotes

There are beautiful and wonderful things to be admire
In the presence of nature
By our true hearts

People who faces any issues
When they doesn't follow
The things that said by heart

Heart is not just made of muscles

It bound by love and emotion
It's alive not only by bloods
But also by emotions and love.

POETRY KHAKHOLIA

नमस्कार, ये है पोइट्री खाखोलिया
गुवाहाटी असम से, बीयालिस वर्ष, कॉन्वेंट एजुकेटेड , शादीशुदा दो बच्चे है। इन्होंने एमकॉम, म.इड, एलएलबी किया है पर लिखना इनकी रुचि रही है स्कूल से ही और अब इसी क्षेत्र में एक मुकाम अर्जित करना चाहती। इन्होंने चालीस से ज्यादा अंथोलॉजी में अपनी लेखनी से नवाजा है और कहानी किताब भी लिख रही है जो जल्द ही आने वाली। लिखना सिर्फ काम नहीं बल्कि जुनून है इनके लिए जो ये हर पल जीती।
आशा है आप सभी को इनकी रचना पसंद आए। Ig:- @hidden_desire_06

ठहराव

इतनी हलचल है
इतनी चहलपेहल है
इतनी भागदौड़ है
लोगों का खुंबा लगा है।
इतना शोर शराबा है।

बाहर इतना शोर है
और भीतर खामोशी है
उस खामोशी में भी एक शोर है
जो क्यूं नहीं कोई सुन पाता
कोई मेहसूस कर पाता...

और उस खामोशी भरे शोर में
मैं कितनी अकेली हूं, तन्हा हूं
उजड़ी वीरान सी मेहसूस करती
जाने क्यूं कोई इस मायूसी का हिस्सा नहीं
शोरगुल जश्न का हिस्सा तो सब बन जाते
पर दुख अकेलेपन का कोई साथी नहीं।

तब क्यूं तन्हा छोड़ जाते
तब क्यूं बेगाने हो जाते
जब साथ सिर्फ सुख का हो
तो अच्छा ही है ऐसे
साथ से हम दूर ही सही,
अकेले सही, पर है तो
अब खुद के साथी
जीवनसाथी ना सही।

By: पोईट्री खाखोलिया

TAHREEM AFZAL

Her name is Tahreem Afzal. She has done her MS in Mathematics. She is also the author of "My Soul's Cravings". Besides being a dream hunter, she is the girl who is traveling on the path called 'life'. She doesn't complain for the obstacles, she just makes sure that her faith never gets blurry, as this is the only candle of light which keeps her going in dark nights.
Ig:- @ Reemsays789

WAIT MY LITTLE ANGEL

Wait my little angel;
your time is yet to come.
Until then, you can rest,
and see the sky changing colors,
and see how winds turn the tides.
Make yourself prepared
for your final flight.
Lessen the burden of your wings.
Let them feel the breeze,
penetrating through the pores,
and when the time will arrive,
trust me you will rise to heights,
and you will shatter all the doubts
that once had grasped your soul.
You will be way above your fears
like a conqueror wining all the battles
in the times when failures were haunting
the fragile existence of yours.
You will be a single colored rainbow;
spreading all over the sky,
making all the other colors envious
of your unbeatable sufficiency.
Wait my little angel,
your time is yet to come.

AAYUSHI KHEDIA

Co-author Aayushi Khedia is a student from Purulia, West Bengal. She can't express much and that is the reason why she started writing. She believes sometimes words speak. Through her shayaris, she tries to express her feelings. She is not a writer by profession but writing is her passion. She wrote her first shayari when she was 9 yrs old. She still remembers that day. Firstly she gives the credit to her mom. Her mother is an exceptional writer but is not famed by others. She thanks 'Your Quote' too that gave her a platform to flourish her writings. She wants to thank her father who always supported her. She wish that he could see this and is determined to make him proud one day. She always try to write not for fame but for the love of her readers. Ig:- @ dazzling_aayu

कभी कभी लफ्ज़ों से ज्यादा चुप्पी की आवाज़ है,
भावनाएं शब्दो की नहीं समझने वालों की मोहताज़ है।
अंदर ही अंदर रह जाती है बातें सभी,
मुश्किल होजती है बितानी रातें कभी ।
लफ्ज़ों का अकसर निकाल लिया जाता है गलत अर्थ,
मैं भी समझ चुकी है की इस दुनिया में बोलना ही है व्यर्थ।।

SRIJA SADHUKHAN

Srija Sadhukhan is 19 years old girl studying BSc Biotechnology in Amity University Kolkata. Love to write poetry and a book worm too. Ig:- @ Syncopatemysuccess

SILENCE

Sitting beside the window sil
Some thoughts roaming around my head
Want to get rid off
But couldn't find a place for silence
Finding silence in every corner of my heart
But couldn't got responses
And my mind was in peace
My heart want the silence of my mind
Here also confusion
Where to find silence in this world?
So much conflict between mind and heart
I want to run away from this fake world
But couldn't as I am living in reality
It's not possible to deny the reality
And again started adjustment to live
In this world of war without silence and peace.

ANKITA MISHRA

I am Ankita Mishra from Cuttack, Odisha. I am a student pursuing my graduation in bachelor's of commerce. Writing was never my passion nor my hobby. All I loved was singing, crafting and playing badminton. Then when I used to stay alone I used to write my feelings no matter happy or sad. And that's how I started writing by expressing my thoughts, feelings and emotions into words. I just hope and look forward towards taking this habit as my passion. Ig:- @the_imperfect_writer_08

When a heart starts to speak,
even the mind goes silent.
It can calm every rising storm,
no matter even if it's violent.

When a heart takes decisions,
it ends us giving two consequences.
Either it goes against the mind,
or goes beyond every expectations.

It can absorb thousands of poisons,
yet will always speak good.
No matter how much it gets hurt,
still it always helps to stand bold.

It's said that our heart is weak,
but little did you know it's strength?
If it goes weak in emotions,
can also stay firm in every difficult situation.

It's the heart that has to
go through various of tantrums,
Yet it's always less cared
and left all alone.

DEESHA SONI

Deesha Soni..a Post Graduate and M.phil adorns the hat of a multitasker of an educationist,artist,poet,photographer,author , blogger,homemaker,wife and mother... She has 10 years experience in the field of Education as a Professor and Coordinator.Deesha has various publications to her credit in national and international levels.
Deesha has various published works to her credit... she has two books published on Amazon... named 'Just thoughts' and 'Random thoughts on pandemic'..Kindle edition and more than 100 plus published works on various online platforms of .. Deesha has been twice nominated for Author of a week award by Storymirror and has also won various recognitions in penning stories and write-ups.. at National and International levels... Deesha has various published works to her credit... she has two books published on Amazon... named 'Just thoughts' and 'Random thoughts on pandemic'..Kindle edition has also won many prizes in National and international levels in many write-ups... Deesha has also published her works in 300 plus anthologies of multiple genres... Ig:- @Deeshagauree

Heart...

My heart is little though...
In it intense emotions flow....
Small tiny petty heart...
Collects love in it's cart...
It beats and palpitates...
And love it perpetually celebrates...
My little heart feels the flutters..
And sweet pain in it.... utters...
Fly my heart fly up....and glide...
For love resides in... which you can't hide...,

ANKITA NAHAR

#AKII#@@@ अंकिता नाहर मूल रूप से अजमेर, राजस्थान की रहने वाली हैं। ये लिखने के लिए हमेशा उत्साहित रहती है साथ ही हमेशा शब्दों से सुकून सा पाती हैं। ये अपने विचारों और जो भी इन्होंने अपनी जिंदगी से सीखा है, अनुभव लिया है उसे अपनी रचनाओं में लिख देती हैं। इससे इनकी रचनाएँ बहुत ही ज्यादा भावुक भावों वाली और प्रभावशाली बन जाती हैं। जो कि पढ़ने वालों को बहुत आकर्षित करती है। वह इस माध्यम को और आगे तक ले जाना चाहती हैं। आप इनकी रचनाओं को इंस्टाग्राम @naharankita1 पर पढ़ सकते हैं।

हां मुझे उससे प्यार था,
प्यार हैं और ये प्यार हमेशा रहेगा

प्यार किया था,
उससे कोई मजाक नहीं किया था।

हां माना अब पहले जैसी बातें नहीं होती,
तो क्या हुआ यार

अक्सर खामोशी से
भी तो प्यार होता हैं।

हां माना अब पहले जैसी
मुलाकातें नहीं होती,

तो क्या हुआ यार,
अक्सर तन्हाई से भी तो प्यार होता हैं ।
©AKII#@@@

DR. ADITI DEV

Hi, Myself Dr Aditi Dev I am a homeopathic& I have done MBA in Hospital Administrations.She is not a writer professionally but she love to share her thoughts in the form of Anthology.She has interest in singing & Drawing also. She loves to visit natural places. Ig:- @ Aditi.dev.509

"चुप सी तन्हाई"

कुछ कमी सी है कुछ नमी सी है,
ये पलकें थोड़ी भीगी सी है।

लफ़्ज़ चाहते है कुछ कहना तुमसे,
मगर दिल में एक कसक सी है।

कैसी ये जुदाई है हमारी,
दिल में दुहाई एक नज़र की है।

लगता है अधूरा सा ये पल,
तुम्हारे बिन हर पल खाली सा है।

ख़ामोश है लफ़्ज़ ओर ये नज़रें,
कहे भी किससे यंहा सब पराया सा है।

है सन्नाटा दिल के हर कोने में,
दिल की हर धड़कन भी टूटीं सी है।

है बेरुख़ी सी हवा में भी,
साँसे भी अब बेवफ़ा सी है।

नज़रें भी अब कह रही है ख़ुद से,
मत रो अब अश्क़ भी सूखे से है।

कैसे बीते ये तनहा दिन,
जब हम थे मगर तुम ना थे।

उदासी सी छा गयी है मन में,
ख़ामोशी सी रहती है दिल में।

तुमसे ही दिन ओर रात है,
तुममें ही ये ज़िन्दगी सिमटी है।

काश आ जाए वो ख़ुशी फिर,
तुम ओर मैं फिर हम से हो ।

PRIYA SINGH

Priya Singh is born & brought up in Dewas, MadhyaPradesh.She's a Proud daughter of her Father B.N.Singh (T.I.).She's completed Masters of Computer Science.She is a Former Educationist, Communication Trainer & Avid Reader.

She's the Co-Author of the Anthologies:-

"It's all about two phase : love & hate" ,"Words From Heart", "Fierce, Fearless N Flawed" & "In the way of borehole", "Unseen Blessings & "Sublime Love", "Mere Papa". All are available in Amazon.

Till today, She's worked in 230+ Anthologies as a Co-Author & compiling 5. Her writing keeps her at ease.

She mostly write quotes on thoughts.

She loves inspiring young minds.

Instagram id- instant__thoughts_

I have my reasons,
to miss you in seasons,
the way you hold my hand
it lets me free from delusions,
Helping hand you stayed
always said, I'm here,
All my peace within You,
Seeking You as seeking Me,
I mostly found myself in
thoughts of You,
When you became
my silence, even I
didn't knew.

GAJAL TAYAL

Gajal is a girl of her own world with a lot of dreams in her eyes. She is a medical student and soon became doctor. She love to write and want to explore world. She is a coauthor in 150+books and compiler of book "love and pandemic ". Ig:- @ gajal27

Heart Saying's

The heart says a lot
You just need to listen it.
It gave signs
You just have to find it
It loves
You just have to maintain it.
It make you fall in love
You just have to make difference
It just attract towards what you like
You just have to sure about it.
It says a lot
You just have to listen it...

YOGESH GURJAR CHINU

इनका नाम योगेश गुर्जर है और निकनेम चीनू है, यह उत्तरप्रदेश के गौतम बुद्ध नगर जिले से है। इन्हें थॉट्स लिखना और पढ़ना बहुत पसंद है, पोएट्री और कोट्स 1300 से ज्यादा लिख चुकी है। 430 Anthology में Co-author के रूप में लिख चुकी है। इनकी पहली सोलो बुक जिसका नाम (सच्ची बातें "चीनू") है।

Ig:- @yogeshgurjar369

Title - दिल की बातें

दिल की बातें दिल ही जाने,
और कोई क्या इसको पहचाने,

दिल में ही बसते है इसके दीवाने,
बाकी सब कुछ न जाने,

कहाँ किसका ठिकाना,
मोहब्बत ही जाने,

आँखों में किसको बसाना,
दिल ही जाने,

छोटे से दिल में गम बहुत है,
जिंदगी ने जख्म दिये भी तो बहुत है,

दिल को हर दर्द से आबाद रखते हैं,
अब बस कुछ बातें ही याद रखते हैं,

खुद को खुद में इस तरह व्यस्त रखते हैं,
कि खुद को खुद में ही मस्त रखते हैं....!!

KAJAL BHARGAV

Kajal bhargav from Lucknow Uttar Pradesh and she's like to writing reading books and Listing music she's want to become a professor and writer.her dream is orphanage homes.

Ig:- @Kajal bhargav2897

]

don't underestimate yourself.....

Never consider yourself less than anyone.
You have to understand your existence first.
don't waste your today worrying about tomorrow
just listen to your heart,
don't be afraid of your shortcomings.
you can do all that you can think nothing is impossible
for you. Don't ever
explain yourself to anyone.
Don't try to be someone else to show what you are.
You are strong but don't be afraid of anyone.
you are god's creation. Only God judge you ,no one
else, just bow down in front of the same God or lay
your head
at the feet of your parents.and Never give up.

SHRUSHTI SUMAN

Srushti Suman living in Bhandara, Maharashtra. She has a degree in computer science and Master of computer application. She seeks happiness in everything, because she thinks life is too short to get upset. She likes to express her own thoughts into words. She like to travel, photography and she passionate for painting. IG : @little_writer_feelings

एक रोज की बात है, खामोशी से सुनना, यह दिल की बात है
मेरा भी दिल धड़का था जब पहली बार उसको देखा था
हजारों की भीड़ में एक वही सच्चा लगा था
जब उसकी ख़ामोशी में मेरी खामोशी को ढूंढा था
हां मुझे भी प्यार हुआ था

इजहार ए मोहब्बत करना था पर लफ्ज़ मिले नहीं
दिल का हाल बयान करना था पर होंठ हिले नहीं
क्या खूब कहा है किसी ने मोहब्बत लफ्जों की मोहताज नहीं
अक्सर आंखें बयान करती है दिल की दास्तान

वह हमारी पहली मुलाकात थी जिसकी गवाह बरसात थी
नजरें मोहब्बत छुपा ना सकी, दिल की बात दबा ना सकी
लेकिन दिल को इंतजार था लफ्जों के इकरार का

शायद कायनात भी हमें मिलाने की साजिश कर रही थी
वहां बिजली कड़की और यहां महबूब बाहों में थी
उस बारिश में भी दिल की तड़प महसूस हो रही थी
वहां खामोशी भी मोहब्बत का इजहार कर रही थी

जब उसकी ख़ामोशी में मेरी खामोशी को ढूंढा था
हां मुझे भी प्यार हुआ था

UNNATI SAWANT

She is a budding and bubbly writer expressing her mind into writing. Passionate to travel round the world exploring and experiencing.

Just Blushing !!

Seeing you love in heart flooding;
Unexpressed emotions are running.

Never knew something beautiful is coming;
Where no one is judging.

World comes closer by hugging;
Everything turns gold by touching.

Sometimes life reality seems nothing;
When your name in ears are buzzing.

By your side rivals seems nothing;
You are just stunning !

KARTHIK N

Karthik N here, published writer and currently pursuing Bachelor's of Business Administration in Parul University, Vadodara in Gujarat. Likes to read and write poems. Extrovert and dynamic. Interact with people who share knowledge. Ig:- @Itz_karthik_n

The survivors of earth
The people rule the earth nowadays
With some disturbance and powerful mace
Going and counting days by days
Living like shoes without lace
Without responsibility and duty
To protect the earth from dangers
Like pollution and deforestation
Itself created by the same humans
Making mistakes again and again
Without learning from it and doing the same
The survivors of earth are enjoying
Their countless and endless days
But it's not the real fact
What they're thinking is just the myth
One day everyone has to leave
That's decided by destiny

www.ingramcontent.com/pod-product-compliance
Lightning Source LLC
Chambersburg PA
CBHW020240250926
51848CB00007BA/489
* 9 7 8 9 3 9 1 4 2 3 7 2 8 *